For Baraka — one of my heroes —E.W.
For Rosemarie —E.F.

Text copyright © 2013 by Eric Walters
Illustrations copyright © 2013 by Eugenie Fernandes

Published in Canada by Tundra Books, a division of Random House of Canada Limited,
One Toronto Street, Suite 300, Toronto, Ontario M5C 2V6

Published in the United States by Tundra Books of Northern New York,
P.O. Box 1030, Plattsburgh, New York 12901

Library of Congress Control Number: 2012955581

Library and Archives Canada Cataloguing in Publication

Walters, Eric, 1957–
      My name is Blessing / by Eric Walters ; illustrated by
Eugenie Fernandes.

ISBN 978-1-77049-301-8. — ISBN 978-1-77049-397-1 (EPUB)

      I. Fernandes, Eugenie, 1943–   II. Title.

PS8595.A598M9 2013   jC813'.54   C2012-908436-0

We acknowledge the financial support of the Government of Canada through the Canada Book Fund and that of the Government of Ontario through the Ontario Media Development Corporation's Ontario Book Initiative. We further acknowledge the support of the Canada Council for the Arts and the Ontario Arts Council for our publishing program.

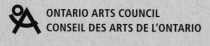

Edited by Debbie Rogosin
Designed by Andrew Roberts
The artwork in this book was rendered in acrylic on paper.
The text was set in Zemke Hand.
www.tundrabooks.com

Printed and bound in China

1 2 3 4 5 6   18 17 16 15 14 13

MY NAME IS
BLESSING

written by
ERIC WALTERS

illustrated by
EUGENIE FERNANDES

TUNDRA BOOKS

Muthini watched his grandmother stirring the big pot. He knew there wouldn't be much to eat. But whatever there was would be shared equally among her nine grandchildren. They lined up, oldest to youngest. Muthini was last. His grandmother — his *Nyanya* — placed a small spoonful on his plate. Using the two fingers of his right hand he scooped up some porridge. It was warm and salty and tasted good as it slipped into his empty stomach.

There was only one thing that would have made it better. He wished that his Nyanya had saved some for herself. Most often, she only ate the burnt parts from the bottom of the pot.

The cousins ate quietly. In truth, they were more like brothers and sisters than cousins. Over time they had come to live with their Nyanya when their own parents had died or left. There was never enough money or food, but Muthini knew his Nyanya did her best. She always gave what she had — extra portions of love.

His Nyanya's name was Mumo — Grace — something she always showed
through quiet and calm acceptance of what fate had given her.
In Kenya, names often mean something. There was his cousin Kioko —
the name given to a child born in the early morning.
And Mueni — born when there were visitors. Mutanu
meant happy, and Mwende, loved.

Muthini's name was hard for him to bear. It meant suffering. That was what his mother had called him before she left. All because he was born with no fingers on his left hand and only two on his right.

His Nyanya never even seemed to notice the missing fingers. It was one of the reasons he loved her so much. Still, Muthini heard the things that were said. Most were spoken quietly, but not always. There were taunts from children and cruel comments from adults. He tried not to let it hurt, but still, it did.

"Nyanya, why *do* I have fewer fingers?"

She glanced up from her work. A thoughtful look came over her face. "We are each given more of some things and less of others."

"I've never met a person with fewer fingers than me."

"Come," she said.

Muthini moved to her side, and unexpectedly she placed her head against his chest. "Yes, it is as I thought. I can hear that your heart is larger than other people's."

"It is?"

"Yes, much larger. That is why you can run so fast."

She stood up and placed her hands on his head. Slowly she nodded. "I was right. Your head and the brains within are bigger than most. That is why you are able to think so clearly."

He *could* think clearly. He was one of the top students in the entire school.

"And I know you have a greater spirit. I can sense it." She paused. "It is so sad that other children only have ten fingers when you have a larger heart, a bigger brain, and greater spirit."

His smile grew from the inside.

"Even if they tease you about having fewer fingers, don't tease them back about what you have that they do not," she said. "Please use your spirit and your head and your heart. Can you promise me?"

"I promise," he said, and wrapped his arms around her.

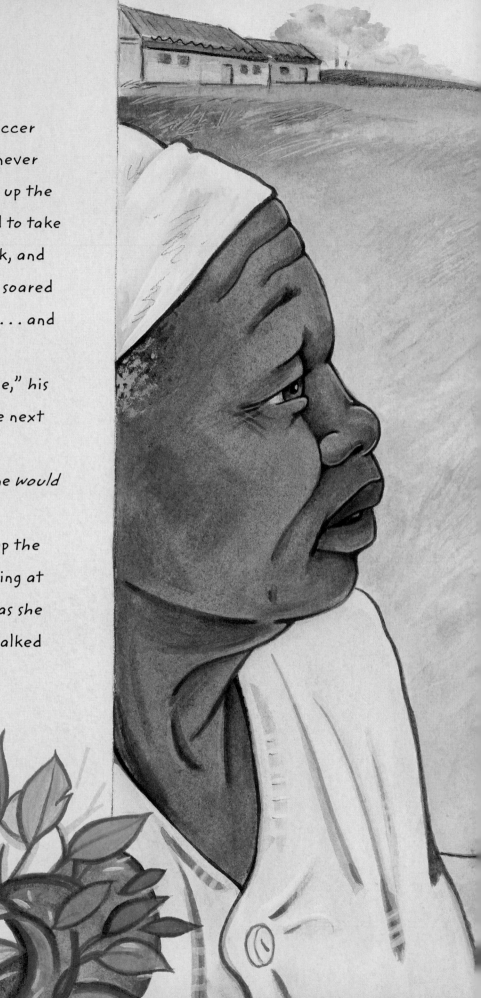

The next day Muthini played soccer with his classmates. The ball never left his foot as Muthini raced up the field, dodging those who tried to take it away. He gave a mighty kick, and everyone watched as the ball soared toward the corner of the net . . . and just missed! He'd shot wide!

"Nobody scores all the time," his cousin Kioko said. "Maybe the next time."

Not maybe. The next time he *would* score.

As Muthini trotted back up the field he saw his Nyanya standing at the school yard fence. Why was she here, so far from home? He walked toward her, feeling anxious.

"You are such a good player, Muthini," she said.

"I didn't score."

"You can't always have happen, what you want to have happen," she said.

He noticed the sadness in her eyes.

"Muthini, it is a long walk to the school for someone as old as I am."

"Nyanya, you are not *that* old."

She reached out and placed a hand on his shoulder. "I am too old to do what I *want* to do. So now I must do what I *have* to do." She let out a deep sigh. "You and I must go on an even longer walk. I only hope you can forgive me."

A single tear rolled down his Nyanya's cheek as she told him her plan. He reached up and, with his two fingers, brushed the tear away. This wasn't what she wanted and it wasn't what he wanted. There were so many grandchildren to provide for and she had so little. And Muthini, the youngest, needed the most. He was too young and she was too old. He felt in his larger heart, understood in his bigger brain, that this was what needed to be done. There was no choice.

They walked along, hand in hand. Muthini's other hand was in the pocket of his tattered shorts. It was a habit he'd gotten into. He wanted people to see him before they saw his hands.

Muthini was working hard to keep his tears inside so he wouldn't upset his grandmother. The walk had been long, and even his young legs felt weary as they trudged along the dusty road.

They stopped at the gates of a little building. There was no sign. Was this the right place, Muthini wondered?

Then he heard the sound of children laughing and playing. Nyanya pushed open the gate and they looked inside. The children were well dressed and they all had shoes. Muthini looked down at his bare feet. His clothing was worn and ragged. He felt nervous.

A man came toward them. He was smiling.

"Hello! My name is Gabriel and this is my home." He gestured around the yard. "*Our home.*"

Muthini looked up at the man. He could see kindness in his eyes.

"You have a very fine home," Nyanya said. "I have come to talk to you about my grandson, Muthini."

Gabriel looked confused. "Why would a child be called Suffering?"

"It was the name given to him before he was left with me."

Muthini could see Nyanya's tears were close.

"I am so old and we have so little. I have come to ask if there is a place for Muthini in your home."

Gabriel gave her a sad smile. "I know how hard this must be for you." He reached out a hand to the boy. "I am happy to meet you, Muthini."

Muthini pulled one hand from his pocket and they shook. Gabriel lifted his hand. Slowly he turned it, looking at where the fingers should have been.

"Let me see your other hand."

Muthini held it out. He felt scared and embarrassed as Gabriel examined it.

Gabriel shook his head. "I am sorry, but there is no room for Muthini in my home."

Muthini was disappointed but not surprised. How could he expect there to be a spot for him when there were already so many children?

"Should I bring him back in a week or two, or in a month?" she asked.

"There will not be room in a week or a month, *or ever*. There will *never* be room for Muthini in my home," Gabriel said.

Muthini's heart dropped. Was it because of his fingers?

"But there is *always* room for a blessing," Gabriel said. "He would be welcome in our home, not as Muthini, not as suffering, but as Baraka, as a blessing."

"You want me to change my name?" Muthini asked.

"I want you to change your *future*," Gabriel replied. "I can never look at you and see suffering and I don't want others to see it either. I want them to hear your name and see what I see, what your Nyanya sees: a blessing. Baraka."

His grandmother smiled. "That is all I have ever seen."

The man held out his hand again. "Hello, my name is Gabriel."

Muthini hesitated, unsure of what to do or say. Then he knew. He held out the hand with just two fingers and took Gabriel's outstretched hand.

"Hello, Gabriel, my name is Baraka . . . and I am a blessing."

BARAKA'S WORLD

Baraka is a real person.

And so is Grace, his grandmother or *Nyanya*.

They live in the Mbooni Region of Kenya, a country in East Africa. Their home is outside the town of Kikima, which is about 150 km (90 miles) southeast of the capital city of Nairobi. It is a rural area in the mountains that can only be reached by rough dirt roads.

Baraka and Grace are members of the Kamba tribe. They speak Kikamba, their tribal language, as well as Swahili, one of the official languages of Kenya. Baraka, along with most school-aged children, also learns English, the country's second official language. Baraka's English is excellent and he loves making jokes and playing with words.

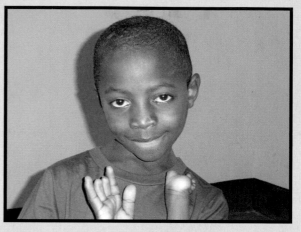

Baraka

Grace (Mumo)

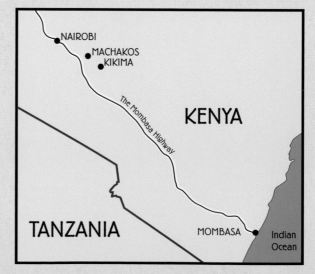

Map of Baraka's Kenya

The first time I met Grace and her grandchildren

When I first met Grace in 2007, she welcomed me with a smile and her hand in greeting. She was caring for nine grandchildren who lived with her in her small hut. In a place where there was so much poverty, they had even less than most.

Grace shared a single bed with the girls, while the boys slept huddled together on rags on the dirt floor.

Often there was only enough for one meal a day. Sometimes, when there was no food, Grace would put a pot of water over the fire to boil and tell her grandchildren, "supper will be coming," hoping they would go to sleep before they realized there was none. Grace always gave them love and caring, but she knew that wasn't enough.

Grace's homestead

The bed shared by all the grandaughters

Baraka's class

Sharing a book with Kanini

Grace's goats, supplied by Creation of Hope

When I travelled to Kenya in 2007, I was shocked to learn about the extent of the orphan crisis there. Parents had been lost to illness, disease, and famine, leaving children completely on their own, or to be cared for by often elderly relatives. I discovered that there were over 500 orphans just like Grace's grandchildren in the Mbooni District alone, a community of only 22,000 people. I decided I had to do something to help.

My family joined with the Kyatha family in Kenya to found The Creation of Hope. This program now provides residential care for 44 children and financial support for 21 children attending high school. It gives ongoing assistance to over 350 orphans in the community who live with extended family, supplying monthly food packages, goats, chickens, school uniforms, clothing, beds, and other items to help in their basic care. In addition, the program funds water projects, provides school supplies and text books to the local school, has founded the only library in Mbooni District, and helped set up a college to teach nursery school staff.

Financial support comes from sponsors in Canada, Germany, the United States, and Kenya, and from the individual donations and fundraising efforts of schools across Canada. One hundred percent of funds from schools goes directly to service.

The newest building — the new Rolling Hills Residence — was completed in 2013. Along with being the home for our orphans, it houses the offices for the program, and has a kitchen, dining hall, and separate conference room that is used by the community.

Residence where Baraka sleeps

At Grace's request, first one grandchild, Kanini, and then Baraka — then known as Muthini — came to live at Rolling Hills Residence. The Creation of Hope continues to provide Grace and the remaining children with monthly food packages, support, and a commitment to fund their high school education. Grace has regular contact with her grandchildren and remains their legal guardian.

Monthly food distribution to orphans in the community

Grace breeds the goats her grandchildren have been given and sells them to The Creation of Hope to be given to other orphans in need. Life for her and her grandchildren has changed from constant desperation to security in the present and confidence in the future.

To find out more about The Creation of Hope, or to get involved, go to the website **www.creationofhope.com**

Baraka singing

Playing in the residence yard

Julia with Baraka

Baraka sees his Nyanya and cousins on a regular basis. He loves playing soccer, spending time with other children in the residence, seeing his family, dancing, and singing. He loves to laugh, and he seems to be friends with everybody. Baraka is a dedicated student who wishes to become an engineer when he grows up. He is sponsored by my daughter Julia and her friend Megan, and his future is bright.

Baraka is a remarkable young man who has a greater spirit than almost anybody I know. He is a source of inspiration and joy, and he is one of my heroes. Baraka truly is a blessing.

Eric Walters
Autumn 2012